GRUMPY BUNNIES

GRUMPY BUNNIES

by Willy Welch
illustrated by Tammie Lyon

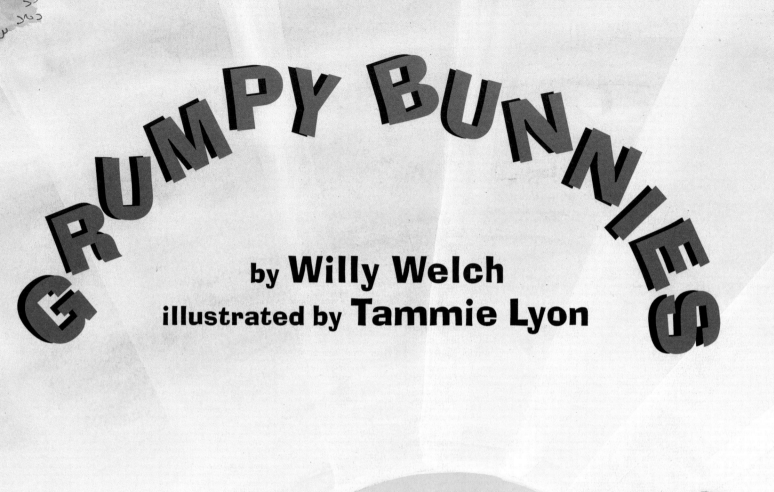

SCHOLASTIC INC.

New York Toronto London Auckland Sydney
Mexico City New Delhi Hong Kong

ISBN 0-439-24943-0

12 11 10 9 8 7 6 5 4 3 2   1 2 3 4 5 6/0

Printed in the U.S.A.   08

First Scholastic printing, February 2001

The illustrations in this book were done in watercolors.
The display type and text were set in Ad Lib.
Book design by *The Kids at Our House*

To Wendy, my favorite morning person
—W.W.

For Kaitie—
my niece, my friend, and always my inspiration
—Aunt Tam

Grumpy Bunnies
in the morning

crusty eyes and groggy yawns

stumble bumbling in the closet
struggle putting school clothes on

Grumpy Bunnies
chomping breakfast
lumpy oatmeal
soggy bread
slumping in their table places
frumpy faces
sulky heads

Grumpy Bunnies
riding buses
knobby seats on bumpy streets

stomping, trudging on the pavement
scuffy shoes and achy feet

**Grumpy Bunnies
on the playground
jungle gymming**

tossing balls

muddy running

grungy sneakers

coming when the teacher calls

Grumpy Bunnies
munching lunches
yummy crumbs of sandwich things

in their classes
learning lessons
numbers
dancing
songs and sings

Grumpy Bunnies after school

huggy mommy

holding hands

tummies hungry cracker snacking

laps and stories

fairy-lands

Grumpy Bunnies bubble bathing

comfy jammies
silky sheets
tucking blankets snuggly kisses
Grumpy Bunnies go to sleep.

**Grumpy Bunnies
snuffle snoring,
flopping in their featherbeds**

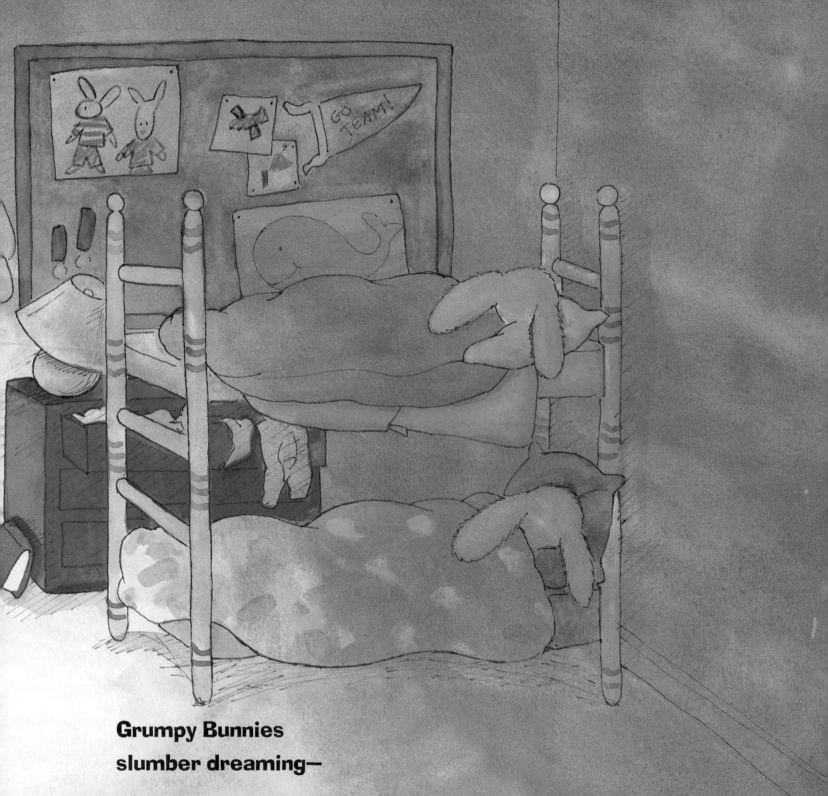

**Grumpy Bunnies
slumber dreaming—**

there's another day ahead.